Ride the Rails WITH THOMAS

Illustrated by Tommy Stubbs

A Random House PICTUREBACK® Book

Random House New York

Thomas the Tank Engine & Friends™

CREATED BY BRITT ALLCROFT

Based on The Railway Series by The Reverend W Awdry.
© 2015 Gullane (Thomas) LLC.
Thomas the Tank Engine & Friends and Thomas & Friends are trademarks of Gullane (Thomas) Limited.
HIT and the HIT Entertainment logo are trademarks of HIT Entertainment Limited.
All rights reserved. Published in the United States by Random House Children's Books, a division of Random House LLC, 1745 Broadway,
New York, NY 10019, and in Canada by Random House of Canada Limited, Toronto, Penguin Random House Companies.
Pictureback, Random House, and the Random House colophon are registered trademarks of Random House LLC.
ISBN 978-0-385-38538-1 (pbk.) — ISBN 978-0-385-38539-8 (ebook)
randomhousekids.com   www.thomasandfriends.com
MANUFACTURED IN CHINA   10 9 8 7 6 5 4 3 2

Some people like to travel in a car.

Some people like to travel in a bus.

Some people like to travel on the water.

Some people like to travel in the air!

But Thomas knows that the best way to travel . . .

. . . is on a train!

The train station is always busy and bustling.

Passengers buy their tickets at the ticket counter.

The ticket tells you everything you need to know.

Train Ticket Memory Match Game

🚂 Have a grown-up help you remove the cards from this book.

🚂 Ask the grown-up to shuffle the cards. Place each card facedown.

🚂 Turn over one card, then turn over another card to see if they match. If they don't, turn both cards facedown again in the same spots. If the cards do match, keep those cards. Continue playing until all matches have been made.

🚂 Play with a friend to see who can make more matches.

Annie and Clarabel are Thomas' coaches. They love carrying passengers wherever they need to go.

Once Thomas is coupled to his coaches, it's time for the passengers to board!

The conductor welcomes the passengers, takes their tickets, and helps them find their seats. Porters carry the luggage.

It's time to depart! Right on Time, Thomas!

Go on a Play Train Trip with Your Friends!

- Place chairs in a line, facing the same direction.

- Use the cards from this book as tickets.

- Take turns playing the conductor. The conductor collects the tickets and helps everyone find their seats.

- Make train noises as the train pulls away from the station. Start slowly, then speed up. *Peep, peep!*

- Talk about what you see out the window as you chug along the tracks.

- When you arrive at your destination, the conductor helps everyone get out of the coach. Where do you want to go next?

Peep, peep! Thomas toots a happy hello as Gordon pulls the Express past.

Thomas stops in Wellsworth. Some passengers get out.
A few new passengers get on board.

It's exciting to ride over the bridge. The view is great!
"Let's play 'I Spy,'" Thomas peeps. "I spy three ducks,
two fishermen, and a cow. Can you see them?"

Thomas arrives at Vicarstown Station. Right on Time, Thomas!

VICARSTOWN

Clarabel

Annie

The passengers collect their luggage and say goodbye to Thomas.

It's always exciting to ride the rails with Thomas!

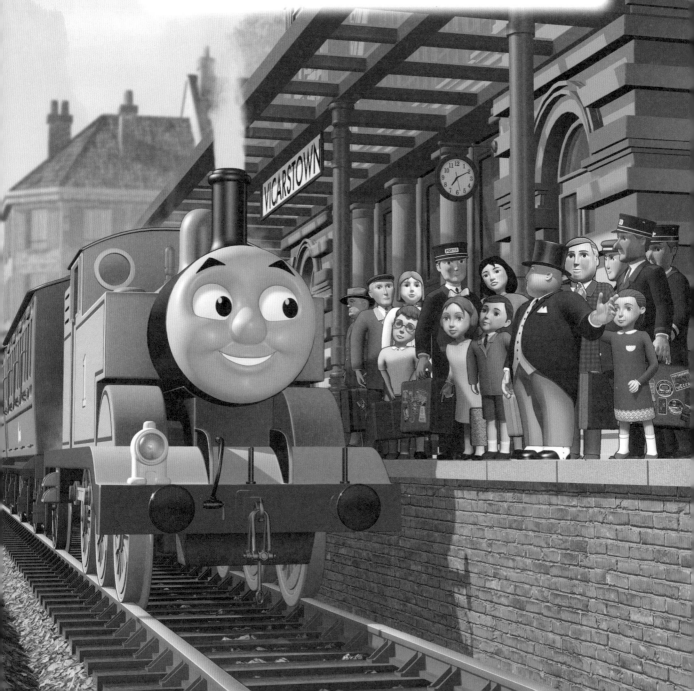

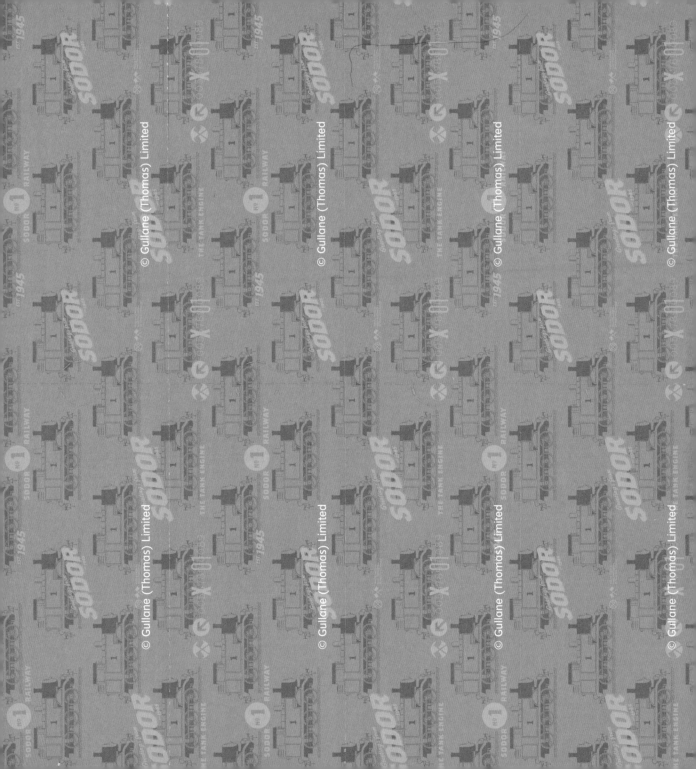

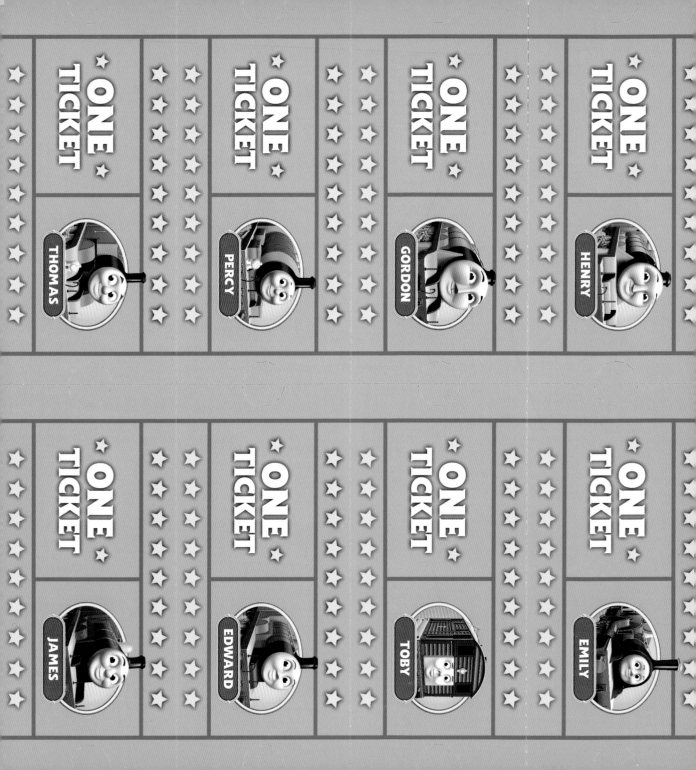

ONE ★ TICKET — THOMAS

ONE ★ TICKET — PERCY

ONE ★ TICKET — GORDON

ONE ★ TICKET — HENRY

ONE ★ TICKET — JAMES

ONE ★ TICKET — EDWARD

ONE ★ TICKET — TOBY

ONE ★ TICKET — EMILY